D0467881

First published 2017 by The O'Brien Press Ltd.
12 Terenure Road East, Rathgar, Dublin 6, D06 HD27, Ireland.
Tel: +353 1 4923333; Fax: +353 1 4922777
E-mail: books@obrien.ie; Website: www.obrien.ie
Reprinted 2017.
The O'Brien Press is a member of Publishing Ireland.

ISBN 978-1-84717-794-0

9 8 7 6 5 4 3 2
21 20 19 18 17

Printed and bound by Drukarnia Skleniarz, Poland.

Sarah Webb was the dlr Writer in Residence 2016–2017.
She worked on this book during her residency.

Dedications –
This one's for my darling niece and god-daughter, Rosie (SW)
To my parents, my biggest heroes Nick and Rosie, and Poppy the dog (SMcC)

Acknowledgements –
With thanks to Ide ní Laoghaire, Nicola Reddy, Emma Byrne and all the O'Brien Press team for their hard work and enthusiasm

Published in:

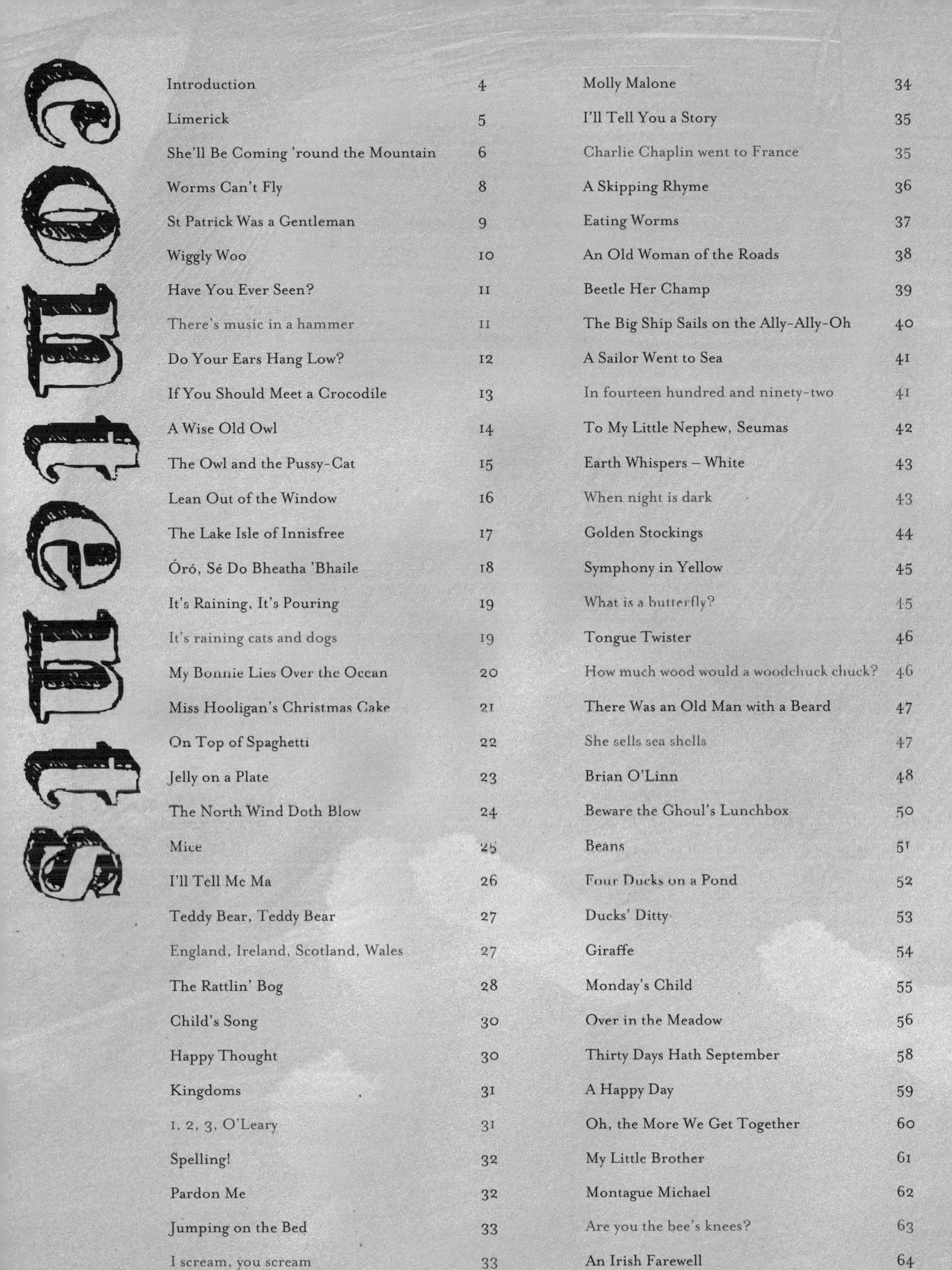

Contents

Introduction

As a child, I loved nursery rhymes and poetry – and I still love them to this day. I have fond memories of sitting on my father's knee as he shared his favourite verses, swaying together to the rhythm of Edward Lear's 'The Owl and the Pussy-Cat', laughing as we twisted our tongues to Peter Piper and his peck of pickled peppers.

In this book I've collected some of my childhood favourites, from traditional Irish songs to street and skipping rhymes, all brought to life by Steve McCarthy's magical illustrations. I also wanted to give children a taste of Irish verse from some of the greats, from W.B. Yeats's iconic 'The Lake Isle of Innisfree' to James Joyce's 'Lean Out of the Window', shortened to suit younger children.

Some of the songs have fascinating backgrounds. 'Miss Hooligan's Christmas Cake' is a version of a popular ballad from the nineteenth century by Charles Frank Horn (the original was called 'Miss Fogarty's Christmas Cake'), which was immortalised by the same Mr Joyce at the tender age of six when he sang it at a concert in aid of the Bray Boat Club in 1888. The song is also referenced in *Finnegans Wake*.

I adore adding *yippee-ayes* and *ye-haas* to 'She'll Be Coming 'round the Mountain', a song that never fails to cheer me up, and I was delighted to discover an Irish connection while researching this book. The woman referenced in the song is said to be Mother Jones, aka Cork-born Mary Harris Jones, once called 'the most dangerous woman in America' for her work in organising strikes for coal miners and railway workers.

I hope you enjoy sharing this book as much as I enjoyed putting it together. And don't forget to add plenty of your own *ye-haas*!

Sarah Webb

Limerick

There once was a small girl called Maggie
Whose dog was enormous and shaggy,
The front end of him
Looked vicious and grim,
But the tail end was friendly and waggy.

She'll Be Coming 'round the Mountain

She'll be coming 'round the mountain when she comes,
She'll be coming 'round the mountain when she comes,
She'll be coming 'round the mountain, coming 'round the mountain,
Coming 'round the mountain when she comes.

She'll be driving six white horses when she comes,
She'll be driving six white horses when she comes,
She'll be driving six white horses, driving six white horses,
Driving six white horses when she comes.

She'll be wearing red pyjamas when she comes,
She'll be wearing red pyjamas when she comes,
She'll be wearing red pyjamas, wearing red pyjamas,
Wearing red pyjamas when she comes.

Singing aye aye yippee, yippie aye,
Singing aye aye yippee, yippie aye,
Singing aye aye yippee, aye aye yippee,
Aye aye yippee, yippee aye.

Worms Can't Fly

Aislinn and Larry O'Loughlin

If worms can't fly,
Then tell me, please,
Why do birds
Wait in trees?

St Patrick Was a Gentleman

Henry Bennett

Oh! St Patrick was a gentleman,
Who came of decent people,
He built a church in Dublin town,
And on it put a steeple.

His father was a Gallagher,
His mother was a Brady,
His aunt was an O'Shaughnessy,
His uncle an O'Grady.

So, success attend St Patrick's fist,
For he's a saint so clever,
Oh! He gave the snakes and toads a twist,
And bothered them forever!

Wiggly Woo

There's a worm at the bottom of my garden,
And his name is Wiggly Woo.
There's a worm at the bottom of my garden,
And all that he can do
Is wiggle all day and wiggle all night,
The neighbours all say what a terrible sight!
There's a worm at the bottom of my garden,
And his name is Wiggly,
Wig-Wig-Wiggly,
Wig-Wig-Wiggly Woo!

Have You Ever Seen?

Have you ever, ever, ever
In your long-legged life
Seen a long-legged sailor
With a long-legged wife?

No, I've never, never, never
In my long-legged life
Seen a long-legged sailor
With a long-legged wife.

There's music in a hammer,
There's music in a nail,
There's music in a tom-cat
If you tread upon his tail.

Do Your Ears Hang Low?

Do your ears hang low?
Do they wobble to and fro?
Can you tie them in a knot?
Can you tie them in a bow?
Can you throw them over your shoulder
Like a continental soldier?
Do your ears hang low?

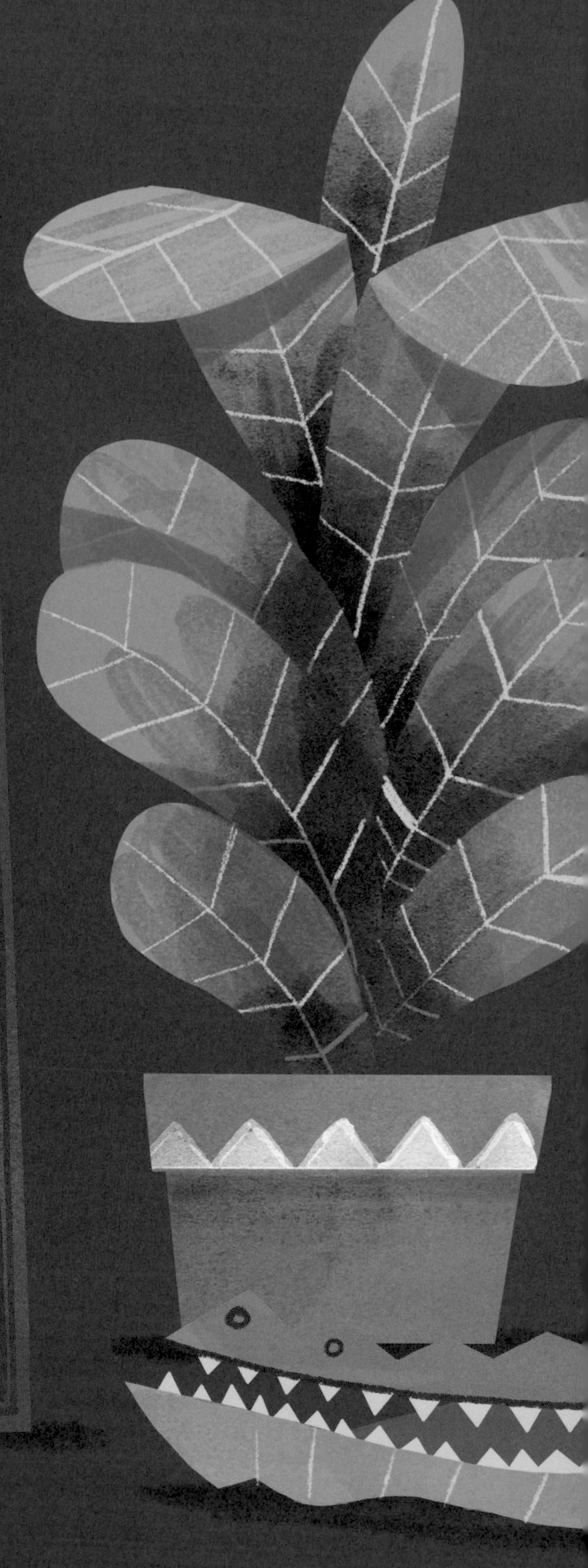

If You Should Meet a Crocodile

Christine F. Fletcher

If you should meet a crocodile
Don't take a stick and poke him;
Ignore the welcome in his smile,
Be careful not to stroke him.
For as he sleeps upon the Nile,
He thinner gets and thinner;
And whene'er you meet a crocodile
He's ready for his dinner.

A Wise Old Owl

A wise old owl sat in an oak,
The more he heard, the less he spoke;
The less he spoke, the more he heard.
Why aren't we all like that wise old bird?

The Owl and the Pussy-Cat

Edward Lear

The Owl and the Pussy-cat went to sea
In a beautiful pea-green boat,
They took some honey, and plenty of money,
Wrapped up in a five-pound note.
The Owl looked up to the stars above,
And sang to a small guitar,
'O lovely Pussy! O Pussy, my love,
What a beautiful Pussy you are,
You are,
You are!
What a beautiful Pussy you are.'

Lean Out of the Window

James Joyce

Lean out of the window,
Goldenhair,
I heard you singing
A merry air.

Singing and singing
A merry air.
Lean out of the window,
Goldenhair.

The Lake Isle of Innisfree

William Butler Yeats

I will arise and go now, and go to Innisfree,
And a small cabin build there, of clay and wattles made:
Nine bean-rows will I have there, a hive for the honey-bee;
And live alone in the bee-loud glade.

Óró, Sé Do Bheatha 'Bhaile

Óró, sé do bheatha 'bhaile,
Óró, sé do bheatha 'bhaile,
Óró, sé do bheatha 'bhaile
Anois ar theacht an tsamhraidh.

Oh-ro, you're welcome home,
Oh-ro, you're welcome home,
Oh-ro, you're welcome home
Now that summer's coming.

It's Raining, It's Pouring

It's raining, it's pouring,
The old man is snoring.
He went to bed and bumped his head
And couldn't get up in the morning.

My Bonnie Lies Over the Ocean

My Bonnie lies over the ocean,
My Bonnie lies over the sea,
My Bonnie lies over the ocean,
O bring back my Bonnie to me.

Bring back, bring back,
O bring back my Bonnie to me, to me.
Bring back, bring back,
O bring back my Bonnie to me.

Miss Hooligan's Christmas Cake

Charles Frank Horn

There were plums and prunes and cherries,
There were citrons and raisins and cinnamon too,
There was nutmeg, cloves and berries
And a crust that was nailed on with glue.
There were caraway seeds in abundance,
Sure it would build up a fine stomach ache,
It would kill a man twice after eating a slice
Of Miss Hooligan's Christmas cake.

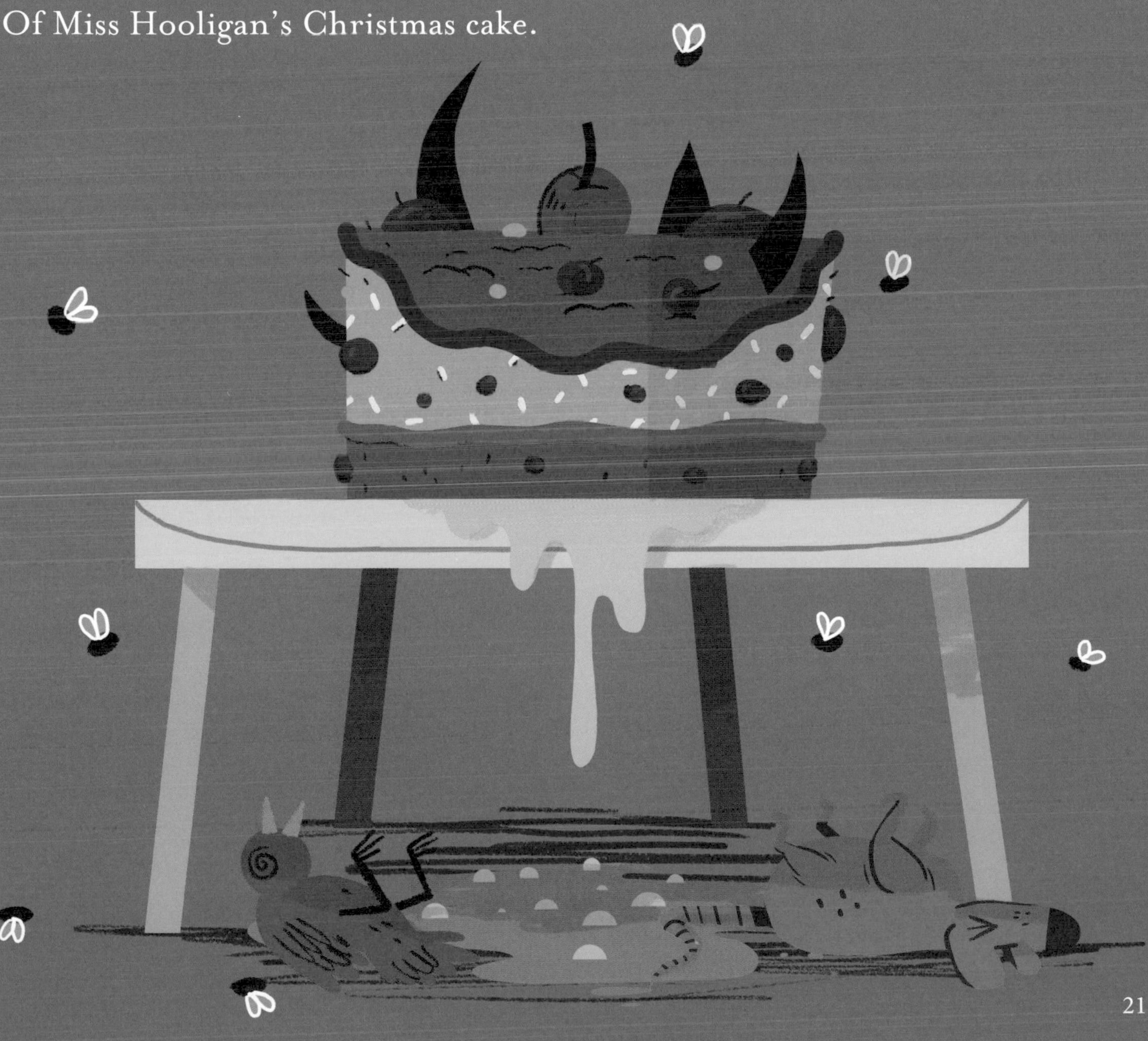

On Top of Spaghetti

On top of spaghetti,
All covered with cheese,
I lost my poor meatball,
When somebody sneezed.

It rolled off the table,
And onto the floor,
And then my poor meatball
Rolled out of the door.

It rolled out to the garden,
And under a bush,
And then my poor meatball
Was nothing but mush.

So if you eat spaghetti,
All covered with cheese,
Hold on to your meatball,
Whenever you sneeze.

Jelly on a Plate

Jelly on a plate,
Jelly on a plate,
Wibble wobble,
Wibble wobble,
Jelly on a plate.

The North Wind Doth Blow

The north wind doth blow and we shall have snow,
And what will poor robin do then, poor thing?
He'll sit in a barn and keep himself warm
And hide his head under his wing, poor thing.

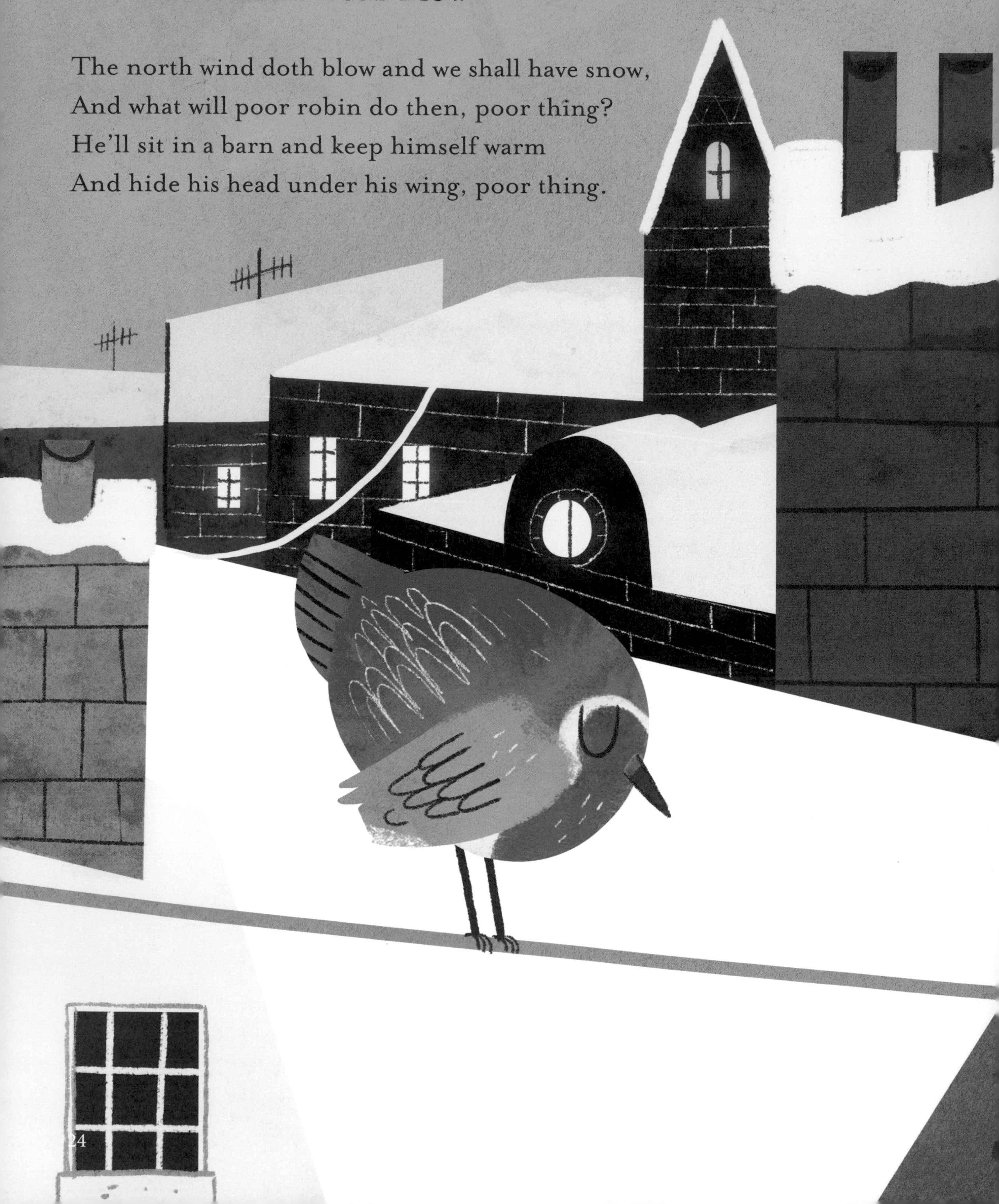

Mice

Rose Fyleman

I think mice
Are rather nice.
Their tails are long,
Their faces small,
They haven't any
Chins at all.
Their ears are pink,
Their teeth are white.
They run about the house at night,
They nibble things they shouldn't touch,
And no one seems to like them much.
But I think mice are nice.

I'll Tell Me Ma

I'll tell me Ma, when I go home,
The boys won't leave the girls alone.
They pulled my hair, they stole my comb,
Well that's alright till I get home.

She is handsome, she is pretty,
She is the belle of Belfast City,
She is a-courtin', one, two, three,
Please won't you tell me, who is she?

Teddy Bear, Teddy Bear

Teddy bear, teddy bear,
Turn around.
Teddy bear, teddy bear,
Touch the ground.
Teddy bear, teddy bear,
Jump up high.
Teddy bear, teddy bear,
Touch the sky.
Teddy bear, teddy bear,
Bend down low.
Teddy bear, teddy bear,
Touch your toes.
Teddy bear, teddy bear,
Turn out the light.
Teddy bear, teddy bear,
Say goodnight.

The Rattlin' Bog

Chorus:
Ho, ro, the rattlin' bog,
The bog down in the valley-o.
Ho, ro, the rattlin' bog,
The bog down in the valley-o.

Now in that bog there was a tree,
A rare tree and a rattlin' tree,
And the tree in the bog,
And the bog down in the valley-o.
Chorus.

Now on that tree there was a branch,
A rare branch and a rattlin' branch,
And the branch on the tree,
And the tree in the bog,
And the bog down in the valley-o.
Chorus.

Now on that branch there was a limb,
A rare limb and a rattlin' limb,
And the limb on the branch,
And the branch on the tree,
And the tree in the bog,
And the bog down in the valley-o.
Chorus.

Now on that limb there was a nest,
A rare nest and a rattlin' nest,
And the nest on the limb,
And the limb on the branch,
And the branch on the tree,
And the tree in the bog,
And the bog down in the valley-o.
Chorus.

Now in that nest there was a bird,
A rare bird and a rattlin' bird,
And the bird in the nest,
And the nest on the limb,
And the limb on the branch,
And the branch on the tree,
And the tree in the bog,
And the bog down in the valley-o.
Chorus.

Child's Song

Thomas Moore

I have a garden of my own,
Shining with flowers of every hue;
I loved it dearly while alone,
But I shall love it more with you.

Happy Thought

Robert Louis Stevenson

The world is so full of a number of things,
I'm sure we should all be as happy as kings.

Kingdoms

Oliver St John Gogarty

The sailor tells the children
His stories of the sea,
Their eyes look over the water
To where his wonders be:
The flowers as big as tea-cups,
The great big butterflies,
The long unfooted beaches
Where stored-up treasure lies.

Spelling!

Mrs **D**
Mrs **I**
Mrs **FFI**
Mrs **C**
Mrs **U**
Mrs **LTY.**

Pardon Me

Pardon me for being so rude,
It was not me, it was my food.
It just popped up to say hello
And now it's gone back down below.

Jumping on the Bed

Five little monkeys,
Jumping on the bed.
One fell off,
And bumped his head.
Mama called the doctor,
And the doctor said:
'No more monkeys,
Jumping on the bed!'

Molly Malone

In Dublin's fair city, where the girls are so pretty,
I first set my eyes on sweet Molly Malone,
As she wheeled her wheelbarrow through streets broad and narrow
Crying, 'Cockles and mussels, alive alive, oh!'

Alive alive, oh! Alive alive, oh!
Crying, 'Cockles and mussels, alive alive, oh!'

I'll Tell You a Story

I'll tell you a story
About Jack a Nory,
And now my story's begun;

I'll tell you another
About Jack and his brother,
And now my story is done!

Charlie Chaplin went to France • to teach the ladies how to dance

Heel to heel, and toe to toe • and all around the GPO.

A Skipping Rhyme

All in together, girls,
It's fine weather, girls,
When is your birthday?
Please jump in.

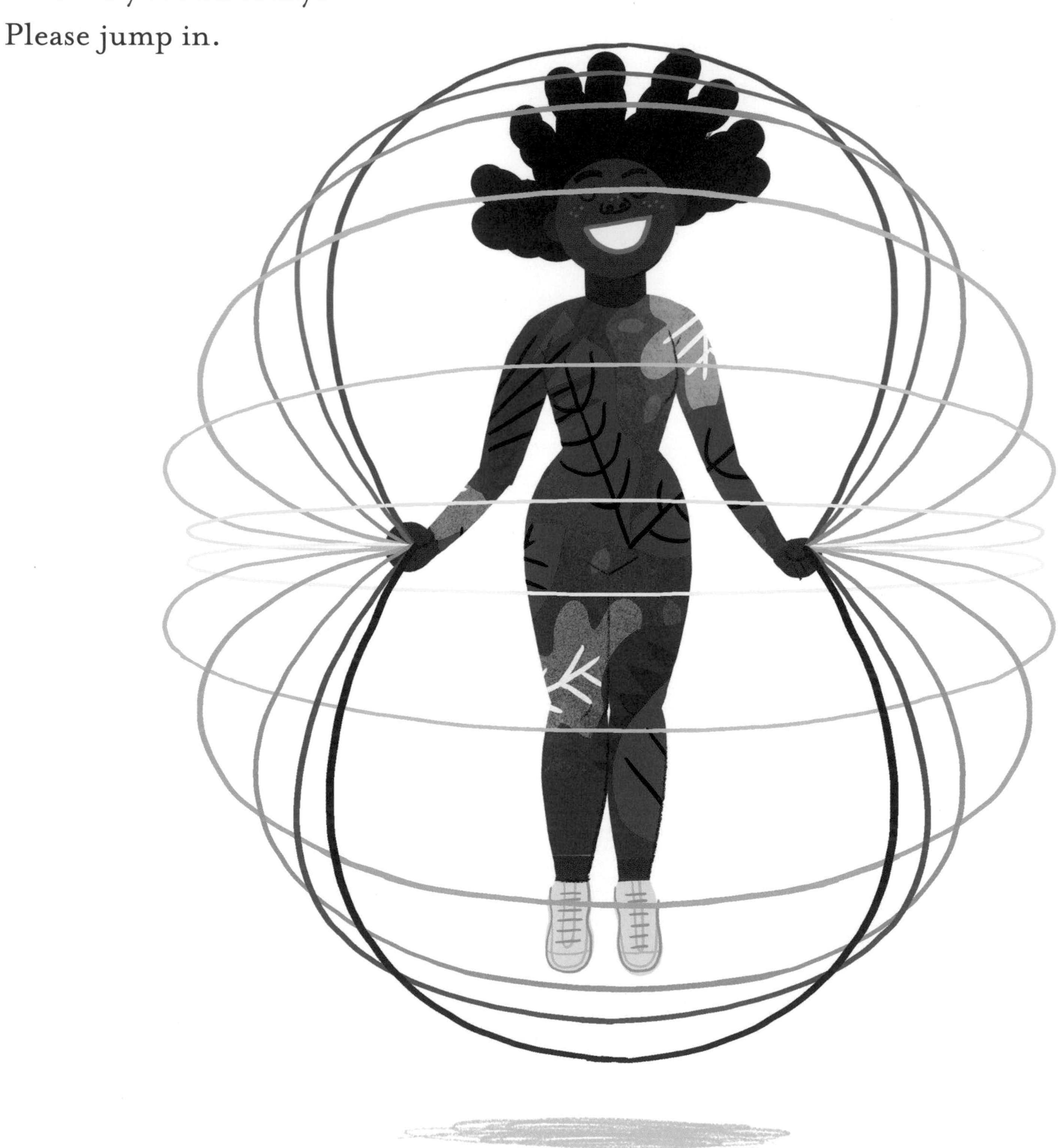

Eating Worms

Nobody loves me, everybody hates me,
I think I'll go and eat worms!
Long, thin, slimy ones,
Short, fat, juicy ones,
And ones that squiggle and squirm.

I bite off the heads, and suck out the juice,
And throw the skins away.
Nobody knows how fat I grow,
On worms three times a day.

An Old Woman of the Roads

Padraic Colum

O, to have a little house!
To own the hearth and stool and all!
The heaped-up sods upon the fire,
The pile of turf against the wall!

To have a clock with weights and chains
And pendulum swinging up and down!
A dresser filled with shining delph,
Speckled and white and blue and brown!

Beetle Her Champ

There was an old woman who lived in a lamp,
She had no room to beetle her champ.
So she up'd with her beetle and broke the lamp
And then she had room to beetle her champ.

The Big Ship Sails on the Ally-Ally-Oh

The big ship sails on the ally-ally-oh,
The ally-ally-oh, the ally-ally-oh,
Oh, the big ship sails on the ally-ally-oh
On the last day of September.

The captain said it will never, never do,
Never, never do, never, never do,
The captain said it will never, never do
On the last day of September.

The big ship sank to the bottom of the sea,
The bottom of the sea, the bottom of the sea,
The big ship sank to the bottom of the sea
On the last day of September.

A Sailor Went to Sea

A sailor went to sea, sea, sea,
To see what he could see, see, see.
But all that he could see, see, see,
Was the bottom of the deep blue sea, sea, sea.

In fourteen hundred and ninety-two,
Columbus sailed the ocean blue.

And I will sing you strange songs
Of places far away,
Where little moaning waters
Have wandered wild astray.

Earth Whispers – White

Julie O'Callaghan

when rain
whispers
it is snow

Golden Stockings

Oliver St John Gogarty

Golden stockings you had on
In the meadow where you ran;
And your little knees together
Bobbed like pippins in the weather.

Symphony in Yellow

Oscar Wilde

An omnibus across the bridge
Crawls like a yellow butterfly,
And, here and there a passer-by
Shows like a little restless midge.

What is a butterfly? At best, he's but a caterpillar dressed.

Tongue Twister

Peter Piper picked a peck of pickled peppers.
A peck of pickled peppers Peter Piper picked;
If Peter Piper picked a peck of pickled peppers,
Where's the peck of pickled peppers Peter Piper picked?

There Was an Old Man with a Beard

Edward Lear

There was an Old Man with a beard,
Who said, 'It is just as I feared!—
Two Owls and a Hen,
Four Larks and a Wren,
Have all built their nests in my beard.'

Brian O'Linn

Brian O'Linn had no breeches to wear,
He got an old sheepskin to make him a pair,
With the fleshy side out and the woolly side in,
'They'll be pleasant and cool,' says Brian O'Linn.

Brian O'Linn was hard up for a coat,
So he borrowed the skin of a neighbouring goat,
With the horns sticking out from his oxters and then,
'Sure they'll take them for pistols,' says Brian O'Linn.

Brian O'Linn had no hat to put on,
So he got an old beaver to make him a one,
There was none of the crown left and less of the brim,
'Sure there's fine ventilation,' says Brian O'Linn.

Brian O'Linn had no watch to put on,
So he scooped out a turnip to make him a one.
Then he placed a young cricket in – under the skin –
'Sure they'll think it is ticking,' says Brian O'Linn.

Beware the Ghoul's Lunchbox

Lucinda Jacob

Look in a vampire's lunchbox;
Lift the lid if you can
On a dripping scream bun
Filled with bloodberry jam.

Look in a witch's lunchbox
And try not to sneeze
Over snail-shell crackers
Flavoured with fleas.

Look in a ghost's lunchbox;
You can eat if you're dead
A see-through mist sandwich
Made from barely there bread.

Beans

Beans, beans, the musical fruit:
The more you eat, the more you toot!
The more you toot, the better you feel,
So beans, beans for every meal!

Four Ducks on a Pond

William Allingham

Four ducks on a pond,
A grass-bank beyond,
A blue sky of spring,
White clouds on the wing;
What a little thing
To remember for years –
To remember with tears!

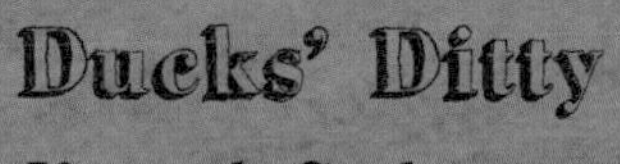

Ducks' Ditty

Kenneth Grahame

All along the backwater,
Through the rushes tall,
Ducks are a-dabbling,
Up tails all!

Giraffe

Aislinn and Larry O'Loughlin

'I wonder,' said the field mouse,
Looking quite perplexed,
'Why is it that all giraffes
Have such enormous necks?'

'I know,' said the barn owl.
'At least, I've heard it said,
It's because a giraffe's body
Is so far from his head.'

Monday's Child

Monday's child is fair of face,
Tuesday's child is full of grace,
Wednesday's child is full of woe,
Thursday's child has far to go,
Friday's child is loving and giving,
Saturday's child works hard for its living,
But the child who is born on the Sabbath day
Is bonny and blithe, and good and gay.

Over in the Meadow

Olive A. Wadsworth

Over in the meadow,
In the sand in the sun
Lived an old mother toadie
And her little toadie one.

'Wink!' said the mother,
'I wink!' said the one,
So they winked and they blinked
In the sand in the sun.

Over in the meadow,
In a hole in a tree
Lived an old mother bluebird
And her little birdies three.

'Sing!' said the mother,
'We sing!' said the three,
So they sang and were glad
In a hole in the tree.

Over in the meadow,
In a sly little den
Lived a grey mother spider
And her little spiders ten.

'Spin!' said the mother,
'We spin!' said the ten,
So they spun lacy webs
In their sly little den.

Thirty Days Hath September

Thirty days hath September,
April, June and November;
February has twenty-eight alone,
All the rest have thirty-one.
Except in Leap Year, that's the time
When February's days are twenty-nine.

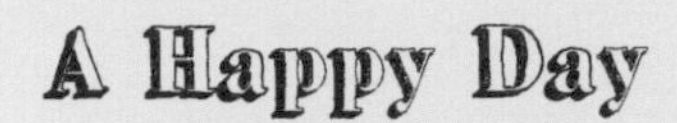

A Happy Day

Alice Taylor

Across the golden amber sand
I watched the sunlit sea,
The waves were sparkling in the sun
And laughing back at me.
Out they danced and in they raced
And tumbled in the caves,
I think that I shall never see
Such happy things as waves.

Oh, the More We Get Together

Oh, the more we get together,
Together, together,
Oh, the more we get together,
The happier we'll be!

For your friends are my friends,
And my friends are your friends.
Oh, the more we get together,
The happier we'll be!

My Little Brother

I have a little brother,
He's only two months old,
He's such a little darling,
He's worth his weight in gold.
He smiles all day at nothing,
He has a dimple on his cheek,
I'm sure he'd say he loved me,
If only he could speak.

Montague Michael

Montague Michael,
You're much too fat,
You wicked old, wily old,
Well-fed cat.

All night you sleep
On a cushion of silk,
And twice a day
I bring you milk.

And once in a while,
When you catch a mouse,
You're the proudest person
In all the house.

Are you the bee's knees or the cat's pyjamas?